KU-758-410

Written by Sue Graves
Illustrated by Jan Lewis
Designed by Blue Sunflower Creative

Language consultant: Betty Root

This is a Parragon book
First published in 2003

Parragon
Queen Street House
4 Queen Street
Bath, BA1 1HE, UK

Copyright © Parragon 2003
All rights reserved. No part of this publication may be reproduced, stored in a retrieval system, or transmitted in any form or by any means, electronic, mechanical, photocopying, recording or otherwise, without the prior consent of the copyright owner.

ISBN 1-40540-059-5
Printed in China

The Great Space Race

A Level 4 Reading Book

p

Notes for Parents

Reading with your child is an enjoyable and rewarding experience. These **Gold Stars** reading books encourage and support children who are learning to read.

There are four different levels of reading book in the series. Within each level, the books can be read in any order. The steps between the levels are deliberately small because it is so important, at this early stage, for children to succeed. Success creates confidence.

Starting to read

Start by reading the book aloud to your child, taking time to talk about the pictures. This will help your child to see that pictures often give clues about the story.

Over a period of time, try to read the same book several times so that your child becomes familiar with the story and the words and phrases. Gradually, your child will want to read the book aloud with you. It helps to run your finger under the words as you say them.

Occasionally, stop and encourage your child to continue reading aloud without you. Join in again when your child needs help. This is the next step towards helping your child become an independent reader.

Finally, your child will be ready to read alone. Listen carefully to your child and give plenty of praise. Remember to make reading an enjoyable experience.

Using your Gold Stars stickers

You can use the **Gold Stars** stickers at the back of the book as a reward for effort as well as achievement. Learning to read is an exciting challenge for every child.

Remember these four important stages:

- Read the story **to** your child.
- Read the story **with** your child.
- Encourage your child to read **to you**.
- Listen to your child read **alone**.

Spike lived on Planet Zed. He lived on Planet Zed with his mum, dad and granny.

Spike also had a robot called Spog.

Every day, Spike went to Space School.
He went with all the other children on
the planet. Spike liked Space School.
Mr Moon was Spike's teacher. He showed
the children how to do lots of things.

He showed them how to float in space.

He showed them how to jump over craters.

He showed them how to turn
head over heels.

But, best of all, Mr Moon showed the children how to fly sky-rockets.

He showed them how to zoom into space.

He showed them how to zip over craters.

He even showed them how to loop the loop!
Spike liked looping the loop best of all.

One day, Spike ran home from school. He was very excited.

"We are going to have a Great Space Race next Friday," he said. "We have to build our own sky-rocket. Will you help me, Dad?"

"Of course," said Dad. "But first, we must draw some plans."

Spike and Dad drew lots and lots of plans.

"Let's build this one," said Spike. "This is the best plan of all."

"Beep, beep!" said Spog.

Spike and Dad built the sky-rocket. They
built it from bits of wire and lots of tin cans.
Spog helped too. Soon it was ready.

"It's the best sky-rocket on Planet Zed,"
said Spike. "Thanks, Dad."

"Now we must think of a name for it,"
said Mum.

"I think we should call it The Super-Looper,"
said Granny.

"Beep, beep!" said Spog.

The next day, Spike tried out his new Super-Looper. Spog went with him.

They zoomed into space

They zipped over craters.

Then they looped the loop.

"Wow!" said Spike. "It's so fast!"

Spog felt very ill.

"Be-eep! Be-eep!" he said.

Soon it was the day of The Great Space Race. The sky-rockets were in line to start the race. A boy called Dak was next to Spike.

"That's a tin can!" laughed Dak. "That will never win the race."

Spike felt very cross.

"It's not a tin can," he said. "It's the best sky-rocket on Planet Zed."

"On your marks…Get set…Go!" said Mr Moon.

Go!

The sky-rockets zoomed into space. They zipped over craters. Then they looped the loop. Spike and Dak were out in front.

"I can see the finish," said Spike. "I must go faster."

Just then, Dak shot past him.

"Oh, no!" said Spike. "Dak is going to win!"

Suddenly, Dak's sky-rocket began to shake a
little. Then it began to shake a lot. There was
a loud bang! Dak fell out and the sky-rocket
landed on the ground with a thump!

Spike saw Dak falling and looped under Dak.
Dak landed in Spike's Super-Looper just as
they crossed over the finishing line.

"We've won! We've won!" said Spike.

Everyone clapped and cheered.

"You were right, Spike," said Dak. "Your sky-rocket isn't a tin can at all. It's the best Super-Looper on Planet Zed."

Mr Moon stuck a gold star on Spike's Super-Looper.

"Well done, Spike," said Mr Moon. "You built a very good sky-rocket."

"Beep, beep!" said Spog.

Answer these questions. Look back in the
book to find the answers.

Where did
Spike live?

What was Spike's
robot called?

Who showed
Spike how to fly
a sky-rocket?

What was the name of
Spike's sky-rocket?

What happened
to Dak?

Who won the race?

Now re-tell the story in your own words.

Gold Stars

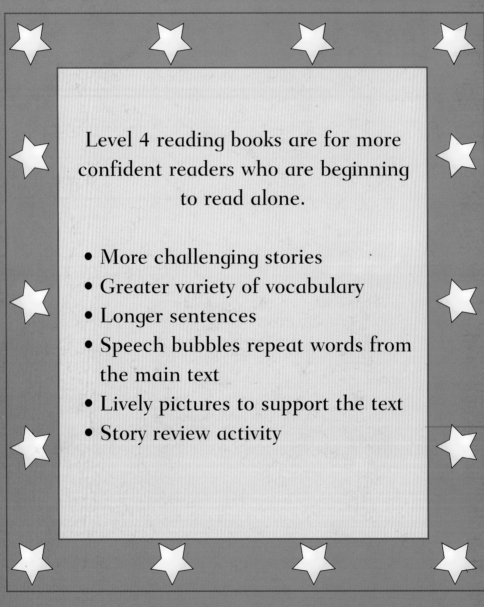

Level 4 reading books are for more confident readers who are beginning to read alone.

- More challenging stories
- Greater variety of vocabulary
- Longer sentences
- Speech bubbles repeat words from the main text
- Lively pictures to support the text
- Story review activity